W9-CNP-141

A Follett JUST Beginning-To-Read Book

The Cookie House

Margaret Hillert

Illustrated by Kinuko Craft

Follett Publishing Company
Chicago

Text copyright © 1978 by Margaret Hillert. Illustrations copyright © 1978 by Follett Publishing Company, a division of Follett Corporation. All rights reserved. No portion of this book may be used or reproduced in any manner whatsoever without written permission from the publisher except in the case of brief quotations embodied in critical reviews and articles. Manufactured in the United States of America.

International Standard Book Number: 0-695-40880-1 Titan binding
International Standard Book Number: 0-695-30880-7 Trade binding

Second Printing

Get up. Get up.
Come with us.
We will go to work.

6

Oh, this is fun.
We can run and jump.
We like it here.

You two play here.
You do not have to work.
We will go now.
But we will come back to get you.

Look here.
Here is something for us.
Something we like.
Have one.

And here is something.
It is little.
It can play with us.

Mother is not here.
Father is not here.
I do not like this.

We can not find the way.

What can we do now?

Who will help us?

I want to go.

We can not go now.

Come down here with me.

14   Come down, down, down.

Get up. Get up.
Look what I see.
Can you see it, too?
Look up, up.

Look at it go.
We can go, too.
Run, run, run.

Oh, see the little house.
I like it.
I like it.
What fun for us.

Look at this and this and this.
I want one.
You can have one, too.

No, you can not.
You can not have that.
It is not for you.

Oh, help, help.
I do not like it in here.
Help me.
Help me.

Here I come.
I will help you.
See me help.

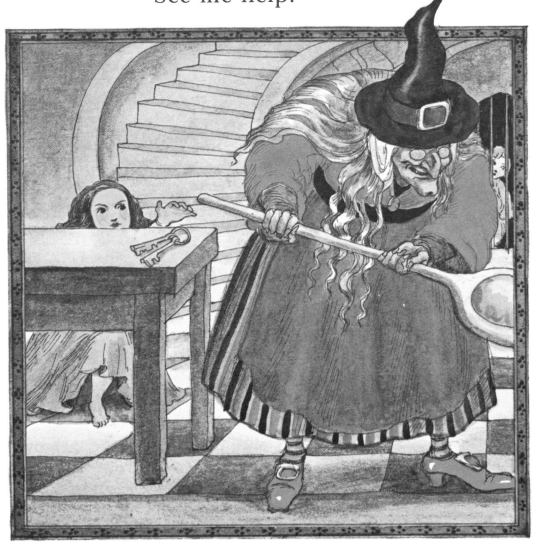

Go in. Go in.
We do not like you.
I will make you go in.
In you go.

23

Come away.
Come away.

Here we go.
Run, run, run.

What is this?
What can we do now?
We can not go in here.

Oh, look at us.
What fun.
What a ride this is!

I see Father.
Father, Father.
Here we are, Father.

The Cookie House

Uses of This Book: Reading for fun. This easy-to-read retelling of Hansel and Gretel is sure to excite the rich imaginations of children.

Word List
All of the 60 words used in *The Cookie House* are listed. Numbers refer to the page on which each word first appears.

7	get		run	**10**	look		home	
	up		and		something	**14**	down	
	come		jump		for		me	
	with		like		one	**15**	see	
	us		it	**11**	little		too	
	we		here	**12**	mother	**16**	at	
	will	**9**	you		father	**17**	house	
	go		two		I	**20**	no	
	to		play	**13**	find		that	
	work		do		the	**21**	in	
8	oh		not		way	**23**	make	
	this		have		what	**24**	away	
	is		now		who	**27**	a	
	fun		but		help		ride	
	can		back		want	**28**	are	